Tinni Pinni Chinni

Tinni Pinni Chinni

(Folk Tales of Himachal)

Santosh Shailja

Ocean Books Pvt. Ltd.

ISO 9001:2008 Publishers

Published by
Ocean Books (P) Ltd.
4/19 Asaf Ali Road,
New Delhi-110 002 (INDIA)
e-mail: info@oceanbooks.in

ISBN 978-81-8430-207-3
Tinni Pinni Chinni
by Santosh Shailja

Edition
First, 2013

Price
Rs. 150.00 (Rs. One Hundred Fifty only)

Printed at
Bhanu Printers, Delhi

With Love

for

My grand children

Kriti, Swati,

Ishita, Garima, Rati,

Shashwat, Kartik

Foreword

Folk tales are expressions of the vibrant life of people - their feelings, aspirations and sense of humour. Their source is not a writer's pen but the people themselves. They are the offsprings of those wise villagers who live life in a very natural way just like the nature around them. Similar is the case with these folk tales from Himachal Pradesh. These embody the simple villagers where romance, humour, cleverness hero-worship etc. reside and find expression in stories that bring smiles as well as tears to the readers. In fact, their utmost contribution is towards humour in life and their rustic touch is wonderful. I, first, wrote them in Hindi. Now I have translated those into English so that English readers, too, may enjoy these. These tales needed to be documented before they got eroded with the passage of time. Though it is an age of science with T.V. and Internet; still none can deny the charm of a bed-side story-book. With this hope, I entrust this book in your hands to make you happy.

– Santosh Shailja

Contents

Tinni Pinni Chinni

There was a house near Chanderbhaga river. It had no other house near it. A few houses were scattered far in the forest. Five persons lived in this house, father, mother, and their daughters named Tinni, Pinni and Chinni. The girls helped their mother in household work and the parents enjoyed themselves with them. But as they grew up, the parents started worrying about their marriages. They talked like this - "How shall we get them married? We don't have wealth to offer dowry in their marriage. Who will accept them without dowry? There is no neighbour with a bridegroom. Oh God! Will our daughters remain unmarried?"

But God was kind enough to listen to their prayer. One morning someone knocked at their door. As Bhola Nath opened the door, he was surprised to see a ram standing there. He said, "Yes, what can I do for you?"

The ram replied with a smile - "Sir, I have come to you for something—in fact, I ask for your daughter's hand in marriage."

"What?" Bhola Nath's jaw opened wide in utter surprise, when he heard a ram speak like a man and its proposal for marriage. The ram said again – "Sir, I already knew that you would be shocked to hear this. But rest assured, I belong to a well-off family and possess good health. I will make your daughter's life happy and comfortable. Moreover, I don't want anything in dowry."

Bhola Nath was too surprised to say anything. He told the ram to sit in the room and went inside to consult with his wife. After much discussion, both agreed to this strange proposal of marriage. Because they knew well that none would come to marry their daughter without dowry. They accepted it as God's will and arranged for the marriage. A nice feast was given to all and Tinni left for her in-law's house with her husband.

This strange marriage was a talk among the people of the village. It was a rare incident. But the couple lived happily. One day a jackal visited the ram and said, "Friend, your happy married life encourages me to get married."

"Why not friend? Marriage has brought me happiness. So get married soon." The ram's reply made the jackal speak – "Then, I need your help to find me a girl as pretty and good as your wife."

The jackal's request made him think about a bride. Suddenly an idea came to his mind. "Why don't you try for my own sister-in-law Pinni?" So he rushed to his father-in-law with this proposal. As Bhola Nath heard this, he and his wife could not agree to this strange match. They could never imagine a jackal to be their son-in-law. But their first son-in-law praised him much and assured them of a marriage without dowry. So Bhola Nath accepted the proposal and fixed a day for another strange marriage. On the appointed day the bridegroom came with his parents and friends and married Pinni. Now, Pinni, too, left with her husband.

Bhola Nath was left with only one daughter now. One day the jackal met one of his friends, a vulture, who was in quest of a bride. The jackal mentioned his beautiful sister-in-law to him. He was so impressed that he requested him to help in his marriage. The jackal approached his father-in-law with a proposal for Chinni. Bhola Nath accepted it as God's will and Chinni, was married to the vulture in no time. So Chinni, too, left for her in-law's house with her husband.

After their daughter's marriage Bhola Nath and his wife felt relieved as well as sad.

One day the wife said to her husband – "It has been long since our daughters left us. We had no news from them. Had there been a brother, he would have gone to meet them. Why don't you visit them and know about their well-being?"

So Bhola Nath got ready to visit her first daughter next morning. As he reached her house, the couple welcomed him heartily. Tinni's house was full of wealth. His son-in-law served him very well. He lived comfortably for one week.

When he got ready to leave, he took his daughter aside and asked – "Tinni dear, you are quite wealthy but I did not see your husband going to work anywhere. I cannot understand your source of income. Where do you get money to buy everything?"

Then Tinni took her father inside a room and showed him a miraculous stone and said – "Father, this is our source of income. My husband hits his head against this stone thrice and gets whatever he wants." Bhola Nath was surprised and made up his mind to get such stone for himself. On his return, he found a similar stone and took it home. When he reached home, he narrated his daughter's well-being to his wife and also showed the miraculous stone to her. She was happy and surprised too. Next morning Bhola Nath got up early and went near the stone. He folded his hands and hit his head against the stone. But nothing came out. He, again, requested for money and hit his head. But instead of getting any money, he got severely hurt and fell unconscious. The wife put him on bed and applied medicine on his forehead. She threw away the stone in great anger. Bhola Nath got well after a week's rest.

Now he got ready to visit his second daughter. As he reached Pinni's house, he was received warmly by his son-in-law. He was pleased to see Pinni leading a comfortable life. The couple entertained Bhola Nath with good food and gifts. But here, too, he was disturbed with this question – "What is my son-in-law's source of income? He does not go to work anywhere." As usual, he enquired form his daughter. She showed him a big brass pan inside the room, and explained – "Father, this miraculous pan fulfills our demands. Whenever we need anything, we put this pan on fire. As it becomes hot-red, my husband brushes its inside with his tail and gets whatever he wants."

After his return, Bhola Nath told everything to his wife. He asked her to put a big brass pan on fire. But she refused in anger. She tried hard to convince him the futility of this proposal. But Bhola Nath was so adamant that he did not listen to her. He had not learnt any lesson from the previous experience. So his wife had to put the pan on fire. When it turned hot-red, he brushed its inside with his beard. As his face touched the pan, it got burnt and he fell unconscious with pain.

His wife was furious with her stupid husband. Cursing her fate, she applied ointment to his face and put him on bed. She threw away the pan to a corner of the room. After a week Bhola Nath started for his third daughter's house. He received a warm welcome by his son-in-law. He was happy to see his daughter very happy in her home. Though they did not possess any miraculous thing, still both worked and earned enough. When Bhola Nath was about to take leave from them, his son-in-law said, "I don't possess much wealth to give you any gift. But I can offer you a pleasure-ride in the sky by my strong feathers."

Bhola Nath was overjoyed at the prospect of flying in the sky. The vulture mounted him upon his back and flew up in the sky. Bhola Nath shouted with joy as he flew over, land, rivers, mountains and cities. He was dazed to fly like a bird. They returned home after flying for the whole day.

After thanking his son-in-law for this wonderful air-journey, he returned home. As he narrated everything to his wife, she was very happy. But when he expressed his resolve to prepare feathers and fly like the vulture, she said angrily – "No, you won't do this foolish act again. None can accomplish another's job." But Bhola Nath was too stubborn to listen to her wise advice. He got into work of making feathers just like his son-in-law. When the feathers were ready, he tightened them on his shoulders with ropes. Now he mounted his wife upon his back and jumped from a hilltop on his maiden flight. But instead of flying up in the sky, he fell down dead along with his wife.

❑

Fruits of Wisdom

There lived a mother with her son in a village. After her husband's death, she brought up her son working hard. When he grew up, she hoped to see him employed and married. She imagined a comfortable life with her grandchildren in future. So one day she gave him one rupee and said – "Son, go and earn a living with this rupee so that I may get you married."

The son said with a smile, "Mother, what shall I earn with one rupee?"

Mother replied gravely – "Son, it is the wisdom, not the rupee, that is capable of earning a living. I have given you one rupee but this advice is worth a lakh which can turn even dust into gold."

The son was wise enough to value his mother's advice. He went out to earn his living. He had his food packed with him. After walking for some hours, he ate his food. As he neared a village, he saw a sweetshop. The shopkeeper had prepared fresh "*Halwa*" (sweet preparation of flour). It spread such a sweet scent, that he was tempted to taste it. He bought "*Halwa*" for one rupee. Now he walked on while enjoying

eating it. A washerman met him on way and said, "Brother, what are you eating? Would you give me a little?"

The boy replied, "Brother, there is a miracle-tree on the far end of this road which has given me this "*Halwa*". You can also get it from there."

The washerman said, "Well, I shall go there but where should I deposit my load of clothes?"

The boy replied, "You can keep it with me and collect when you come back".

The washerman said, "Brother what is your good name?"

The boy replied, "Storm."

After the washerman's departure, the boy put on those clean clothes left by him. He walked on his way and met a horseman. He asked the boy – "What are you eating brother? Would you give me a little?"

The boy replied, "There is a miracle-tree on the other end of this road. I have got this "*Halwa*" from it. You, too, can beg it from it."

The horseman said, "All right, I shall go there. But with whom should I leave my horse?"

The boy replied, "You can leave it with me and get it back on return."

The horseman entrusted the boy with his horse and said, "What is your good name brother?"

The boy replied, "Ishwar."

As the horseman went, the boy mounted on the horse and went to the opposite direction. He met a woman with her young daughter on the way. She said, "Son, what are you eating? Would you give me a little?"

The boy replied, "Mother, I am eating "*Halwa*". If you want it, go ahead. There is a miracle-tree at the end of this road, pray to it and get the '*Halwa*'."

The woman got ready to go there. "But with whom should I leave my daughter?" she asked.

The boy replied, "Mother you can leave her in my care and take her back when you come back."

The woman asked, "What is your name?" The boy replied, "Son-in-law at Home."

As the woman went away, the boy mounted the girl on the horse and galloped away to his home.

After some time the washerman came back and looked for the boy. He could find neither the miracle-tree nor the boy. Exasperated he went to the police station to lodge a complaint. The inspector asked – "What is the name of the thief?"

The washerman replied – "Storm."

On hearing this, the inspector had a hearty laugh "Storm? Well, storm is meant to blow away the clothes." Everyone laughed at the washerman. Now the horseman approached the inspector to lodge a complaint against the thief of his horse.

The inspector asked –"What is the name of the thief?"

He replied, "Ishwar."

The inspector laughed again, "Ishwar means God. Can God commit a theft when everything belongs to Him only?"

The poor horseman felt embarrassed and kept quiet. Then the woman approached the inspector with her complaint. The inspector said – "What is the name of the thief who took away your daughter?"

The woman replied, "Son-in-law at Home."

On hearing the name, the inspector could not restrain his laughter and said, "Mother, go to your home. You will find your son-in-law there."

So the woman, too, went away cursing her bad luck like the washerman and the horseman.

Now the boy reached his home and touched the feet of his mother with his bride and said, "Mother, I acted upon your advice. So I earned enough to bring home a horse and your daughter-in-law." Mother kissed her wise son's forehead and welcomed her daughter-in-law into the house.

❑

Diamond cuts Diamond

There was a clever robber. He robbed in such a way that none could understand his hidden tactics. And he always escaped unharmed. One day he planned to rob a trader. As he reached his house, he saw preparation of a marriage. The trader's daughter was to be married in the evening, so various sweets were being prepared by the cooks. There was an aroma of sweets filling the air. The robber was lured to taste these delicacies. He thought, "Today I would rob sweets in place of rupees. Let me enjoy these mouth-watering *Ladoos* first.

So he approached the Head Cook and said, "Sir my uncle sent me to help you. I know how to prepare the best *Ladoos*..... Please let me help you."

The simple cook believed his words and entrusted him with that job. The robber was indeed an expert in making *Ladoos*. He prepared a basket-full of *Ladoos* and kept it aside. Then he filled another basket with cow-dung, covered it with grass and leaves and spread a few *Ladoos* over it. The basket was sent to the store-

room for the marriage. Now he got one towel and a bottle of honey from the cook. Then he covered the big basket of *Ladoos* with that towel and put cow-dung over it. Showing it to the cook, he said – "Sir, uncle had asked me to hand over this bottle to the doctor. So I'm going to the doctor's shop I will also carry away this basket of cow-dung as it is spreading bad smell."

The cook was very pleased with his proposal. He nodded 'Yes' and let the robber take away that basket. None bothered to check him as everyone was merrily busy in the marriage.

The robber walked homewards smiling and imagining the bliss of eating those *Ladoos.* He felt proud of his cleverness which none could even imagine. But there was one person who was watching him from the very beginning. This person, too, was a robber. So he understood his plan. He followed the first robber. As he noticed him, he asked in anger – "Who are you? Why are you following me?"

The second robber muttered meekly, "Sir I am a mere coolie. I am following you in the hope of some job. Would you let me carry this basket for you?"

The first robber thought, "What's the harm in letting him carry the basket?" So he put the basket on his head and walked ahead. The coolie asked – "Sir, what is in the basket?"

The robber replied angrily, "Why do you ask it – it may be anything? Why does it bother you?" Then, after a while he added very cleverly – "It has the seeds of honey."

"Seeds of honey?" The robber looked towards him in wonder. "Are these seeds of honey? I never knew that honey had seeds."

Now the robber felt embarrassed. He immediately replied – "Oh, stupid, these are the bees that prepare honey so I called these seeds of honey." Now both burst into a loud laughter. The robber felt proud of his cleverness.

The coolie had noticed the bottle of honey too. So he asked – "Sir, what is in the bottle?"

The robber was quick to reply – "Oh, it is poison. Be careful to hold it." The coolie carried it with the basket. As he walked faster, the robber said – "You may wait for me at the tea-shop on the bridge of this road. I shall reach soon. But, be careful and don't open the basket or the bottle, otherwise you would lose your life."

The coolie nodded – "Yes, Sir." and walked forward. As he had walked very fast so he stopped to take rest on the way. Out of curiosity, he uncovered the basket. As soon as the cover was put aside, sweet *Ladoos* were seen underneath. "Ah! What luck!" The coolie exclaimed happily and started eating the *Ladoos* with both hands. After eating ¾ of the *Ladoos*, he packed the rest in a leaf and hid it behind a tree. He filled the empty basket with grass and started on his journey.

He thought of a cleverer plan. As he put the basket down at the tea-shop, he started crying in a loud voice. People gathered around him – "What is the matter?" The coolie replied – "My master had entrusted me with this basket of honey-seeds. But while I passed the forest, all the seeds of honey flew away and now there is no seed left in the basket."

"Honey Seeds?" People laughed to hear him. "You must be mad. There are no seeds of honey." Then the robber, too, reached there. On seeing him, the coolie's cries grew louder. The robber said, "What happened? Why do you weep?" The coolie replied - "Sir, you entrusted me with a basket full of seeds of honey........ Sir, all those bees flew away in the forest and the basket is empty now. I am the culprit—you may punish me for this."

The robber stood shocked. He was cheated by a cleverer robber in broad daylight. He could have beaten him to death for this cheating but he was helpless before the crowd. He was now entrapped in his own words. As he kept thinking over it, the coolie blurted out - "Sir, you may not punish me, but I think myself guilty, so I drink this poison to end my life." In an instant he drank the honey from the bottle. This proved the last humiliating defeat of the first robber.

❑

Clever Pussy Cat

Once, a pet cat was driven out of the house. Poor cat wandered here and there in search of food and shelter. She longed for the good old days when she used to eat bread and milk and sleep on the cushioned bed. Today she had not had even her breakfast. A mare met her on the way and said – "Maussi, you look very sad, why?"

She replied, "My master has expelled me out of the house due to my old age. I am unable to catch the mice. So I have been roaming about hungry since morning."

The mare heaved a sigh and said – "I have the same sad story to tell you. I used to carry heavy loads when I was young. Now being unable to do so, I have been driven out by my master."

Both sufferers walked together. They met a dog on the way. He, too, narrated his tale with tears – "I, too, am prey to this injustice. My master threw me out of the house due to my old age." As they advanced further, a cock stood in the way, croaking.

"Why are you croaking at this odd hour?" They asked the cock.

The cock replied, "My mistress has planned to kill and cook me today. So I am croaking for the last time now."

These three helpless companions took the fourth one with them. They reached a forest. They saw a large house and entered it. It was full of food and other things but devoid of its owner. The cat was clever enough to think of a plan. She instructed the mare to stand on the way and the dog to hide behind the door. The cock was to stand on the wall. After giving them complete instructions, the cat hid herself beside the stove in the kitchen.

As evening fell, the owner of the house entered the kitchen to make fire. As soon as he lighted the stove, the cat pounced upon his hands. He was taken aback with this sudden attack and ran out in panic. Just as he passed by the door, the dog bit him on the legs. He rushed out crying with pain. But the mare gave him a strong kick on the way and he fell down. At that moment, the cock started croaking loudly. This horrified the man and he ran out shouting - "Ghost...... Ghost!!"

Now these four companions heaved a sigh of relief. They had the whole house for themselves. The cat took charge of the kitchen; the mare and the dog were in charge of outside jobs while the cock kept dancing all around. The pussy cat's cleverness provided the homeless companions with home as well as food for life.

❑

Two Fools

Once there lived an old woman with her two sons. They had neither a field nor a job. She used to labour in others fields and make both ends meet. Her husband had died long ago. She exhorted her sons to work with her but they never listened to her. Both were too lazy to share their mother's burden. They were content to live with whatever she could earn. But one day she fell sick. The village *Vaid* was called. He felt her pulse and prescribed her good food with butter because she suffered from acute weakness.

Now both brothers were really worried. They had not had food since her illness. Then how to give her good food with butter? The elder Karma suggested to the younger Dharma – "Let's go to the neighbours and ask for butter to feed our mother."

So Dharma went out while Karma remained with his mother. The villagers took pity on him and gave him a bowl of butter. He returned happily. But when he was walking, he heard the sound of shrubs which grew on both sides of the road. He looked for the source of sound. As he could not see anyone, he understood that the shrubs were making a noise and taunting him. He shouted in anger – "O' shrubs! Be quiet, Don't make a noise." But how could the shrubs stop moving and producing sound? Foolish Dharma could not understand that it was the wind that produced a sound while passing through them. He was beside himself with anger. To quieten them he held the shrubs with his hands and applied butter to them. The shrubs got stuck due to butter and could not move to produce a sound. Dharama was pleased with his success. He applied whole butter over the shrubs and returned home smiling at his cleverness.

When he reached home, Karma asked for butter so that mother may be given butter-tea. Dharama showed him the empty bowl and narrated the whole story. Karma was furious with foolish Dharma. But the problem of feeding the mother was still unsolved. So he thought of going himself. He told Dharma to sit by his mother and went to bring butter-milk and barley-flour from the neighbours. He went thinking about the future when they would also enjoy a meal after so many days. The neighbours were kind enough to give them butter-milk. As he crossed the road, he chanced to see dog's shit lying there. Had he been a wise man, he would have passed it carefully. But he was a fool of the first water. So he shouted at it – "O shit! get off my way. Be off I am in a hurry."

How could dog's shit hear his words? So it remained where it was. Stupid Karma took it for an insult to himself. In an instant he threw the whole buttermilk

over it. The shit was flooded down to the drain. At this Karma felt pleased with his success and went home.

As Dharma saw him, he got up and said, "Brother, come soon, lets give food to mother - where is butter-milk?" Karma showed him the empty bucket and narrated the whole story. Now Dharma cursed his brother's foolishness. Indeed one surpassed the other in stupidity. As the mother had not eaten anything since long, she was sinking down. Her eyes were closed and pulse had slowed. Both brothers could see that she was going to die soon. So Dharma told Karma to go to the temple and bring the priest Lama to recite the last prayer for the mother. He told him to borrow the cooking-pan too from the priest so that they may cook the food for the feast after mother's death.

As he sat beside his mother's bed, he noticed a fly upon her mouth. He immediately made it fly away. But it came again and sat on her mouth. He hit it with his hand but it returned again. The fly, too, was as stubborn as Dharma. Now this was beyond his tolerance. Foolish Dharma decided to teach it a good lesson. He shouted – "O' you Idiot! How dare you touch my mother's mouth? You will be punished for this" – saying this, he hit it with the grinding-stone. As soon as it hit the mother's face, the fly flew away along with his mother's life.

As Dharma saw his mother dead, he was shocked. He had killed her. What would Karma do with Dharma? He racked his brain and thought of a plan. He carried mother's dead body and placed it against the closed door in a sitting position. When Karma came back, he knocked at the door. When none opened it, he pushed it forcefully. The door broke open and he fell down over his mother's dead body.

Now Dharma shouted – "You fool ! You killed our mother. She had got up to open the door and you pushed so hard that the door broke and she was killed." The poor fellow was so overpowered with guilt and fear that he begged his brother not to tell this to anyone. Dharma agreed to his request with a show of kindness. Then he went to the Lama to bring him for mother's last rites. It was a practice in the village that after the cremation, the family serves a lunch to all the villagers. But these two brothers had neither the grains nor the money. There was nothing to cook for the feast. So they thought of a clever plan. Both cut the dead body into small pieces and cooked it in the big pan. When the villagers came to them for consolation, they served them with that meat. People were surprised to see their ability in arranging the feast. They praised them for this.

After having meal, the Lama asked them to take him to their mother's body for the last rites, "But where is the dead body? You have already eaten it" both spoke in one voice.

"What? You served us the meat of your dead mother?" All shouted with horror and anger. They tried to catch them but both took to their heels.

They returned to the village after one month. The villagers took pity upon these orphans and pardoned them. Even the Lama sent them a message that he, too, would pardon them if they returned his cooking-pan.

When Dharma went to the Lama to return his cooking-pan, Lama thought to teach him a lesson. So he let off his shepherd-dog on the way. As the ferocious dog ran towards Dharma, he placed the pan upside down over his head. The pan was so big that it covered his whole body while sitting on the ground. The dog ran around the pan barking but could not harm him. He sat smiling inside the pan. He had his pocket-knife and made small cuts in the pan with it. At last the Lama took pity on him and called back the dog.

When Dharma reached the Lama's place with the cooking-pan, he was enraged to see the pan. It was spoiled with holes all round. "Why are there holes in the pan? You have destroyed it? Who did It? It must be your doing." The Lama shouted in anger.

"No, Sir it is not my doing but of your own dog. I was sitting inside the pan scared of your dog. It was the dog which ran around the pan biting it with its teeth and paws."

The Lama felt sorry for his own blunder while Dharma returned smiling at his cleverness.

❑

Imitation needs Intelligence

Once a fox and a rabbit lived in a forest together. They went for hunting and shared their food together. One day they could not get anything to eat. They had been roaming about since morning and it was evening now. They were dying of hunger and thirst. Suddenly the fox saw shrubs of berries at a distance. He ran towards it and shook them so hard that the berries fell on the ground in a heap.

"Now eat to your fill, friend. I will eat to my heart's content and go to sleep here. I won't go farther now." the fox spoke merrily.

The rabbit replied – "It is right to eat berries but wrong to sleep here."

"Why? What is wrong in sleeping here? I am not going from here." With these words the fox lay down to sleep after eating. But the rabbit did not like this. He disliked this laziness of his friend. He was wise enough to know that one should save something for future and make a permanent arrangement. So after eating berries, he continued his journey. He found a

broken plough and a rope on the way. He carried these things. He noticed a drum and a pot of curd too. He picked up these too and reached a cave. The cave was closed with a big stone at the entrance. He pushed away it and entered it. He was surprised to see it full of enough food and other things. As he settled down happily, a thundering voice came from outside - "Who is in?"

The voice made the rabbit tremble to the bone. He understood that it must be a demon. But he gathered his wits and replied with full force - "I am the Grand Demon who can beat you hard."

The demon was startled and asked "Who can be stronger than me? Show me your teeth?"

The rabbit's sharp brain was in motion. He immediately threw out the plough. The demon saw the plough and wondered - "Such big teeth? "

He, again, thundered - "Show me your moustaches."

The rabbit threw out the rope. The demon's jaw opened wide - "Oh! So big moustaches."

But he tried again - "Show me your spit."

The rabbit threw out the curd.

"So much spit!" the demon was now really afraid of his stronger enemy. He tried for the last time - "Just beat your Tummy". The rabbit beat the drum with full force. The sound resounded in the forest. Now the demon took to his heels in great fear.

The rabbit heaved a sigh of relief. But he knew that the danger was not over yet. The demon will return next morning and then the rabbit won't be able to face his might. So after spending the night he left early in the morning with a bag of food. The fox met him on the way. He said, "Friend, where did you get so much food?" The rabbit narrated the whole story to him. The fox, too, wanted to try his luck at the cave. He repeated each and every detail in his mind and entered that cave.

The demon came and shouted – "Who is in?"

As the fox heard the demon's voice, he was shaken to his feet. Fear overpowered him. As his wits failed, he forgot the answer. In a trembling voice he muttered – "I am a fox and have come to eat you up." No sooner did the demon hear these words, he rushed in and pounced upon the fox. The foolish fox was eaten up in no time.

❑

Fortune's Smile

Binwa and Hinwa were two brothers. Binwa was the elder one while Hinwa, the younger one. Binwa was cleverer than Hinwa. He made him work in the fields and look after the cattle while he enjoyed himself. Hinwa was so simple-minded, that he did not understand his brother's tactics. But he felt very sad to get only dry *rotis* for all his hard-work.

One day he went to the fields early as usual. When he started ploughing the field, he remembered that he had forgotten to bring the basket of seeds. So he went back to home. As he entered the house, his brother and sister-in-law were not at home. But there was an aroma of good food filling the house. He went to the kitchen and was surprised to see a variety of dishes alongwith *Paranthas* and *Kheer*. He failed to understand the reason as it was not a festival-day. Was it prepared for some guest? For whom are these prepared? He had never tasted such nice dishes. As he sat thinking, he understood the whole matter slowly. It was the daily routine of his brother and *Bhabhi*. Both of them enjoyed

all these delicacies after sending him to toil down in the fields. At this, his heart became heavy with sorrow. He laboured for them as his own family while they treated him just like a hired servant. It was too cruel to bear. He lost all interest in life and felt like leaving them forever.

He returned to the fields and kept working without interest. When he came back in the evening, his *Bhabhi* served him the usual dry *rotis*. He could not control his feelings and said – "Bhabhi, today you have cooked good dishes with *Paranthas* and *Kheer*. Then why these dry *Rotis* for me? Why?

Bhabhi was startled at his question because Hinwa had never asked this before. Binwa was sitting nearby. He replied with a malicious sneer – "Hinwa, the reason is that your fate is sleeping across seven seas. As long as your fate keeps sleeping, you will have to live by these dry *Rotis* only."

Hinwa did not utter a single word. He left the *rotis* and the house too. His brother tried hard to stop him but he could no longer bear their injustice. He had realized the truth that he had to go in the quest of his destiny.

As he started his journey, he reached a forest. Suddenly his eyes fell on a snake which was moving towards a nest of eggs on a tree. Hinwa aimed at the snake's head with a stone and saved those eggs. As he was too tired to step further, he lay down under that tree to rest. As the vultures returned to their nest, they looked at the dead snake and the young boy.

They understood the whole matter. They thanked him for saving their eggs. In answer to their query, Hinwa narrated the sad story of his life. The vulture said, "It is very difficult for you to wake up your fate after crossing seven seas. So let us help you by mounting you on our back. We will fly you to your destination." Hinwa was very pleased by their proposal. So they started on their journey. They met a dry tree on their way. It stopped them with this request – "Please ask my fate, too, why do I always remain dry while other trees flower in spring?"

The vultures kept on flying over seven seas and reached Hinwa's destination. His fate was, indeed, fast asleep there. Hinwa woke him up and requested to smile over his bad-luck. Fate acceded to his request. Then Hinwa asked it about the reason of the bad-luck of the dry-tree. Fortune told him that there was hidden wealth under the root of the tree that is guarded by a snake. If you kill the snake and dig up all the wealth, the tree would bear new leaves and you would also become wealthy. Hinwa returned happily. The vulture flew him safely across seven seas. As he reached the dry tree, he killed the snake hidden under the root and had all the wealth. Now the tree smiled with green leaves and Hinwa was a rich young man. As he passed a state, he heard an announcement – "Whoever would cure the sick princess, can earn a precious reward."

Hinwa went to the King's palace. He had knowledge of some life-saving drugs. He prepared medicine out of some herbs and gave it to the princess.

By God's grace, the medicine proved miraculous and the princess recovered fully. The King was so pleased with the young boy that he requested him to be his son-in-law. So Hinwa got married to the princess and now his life really became blessed with good Fortune. ❑

In the Land of Giants

There lived a naughty boy in a village. He always played tricks with everyone. So he was called by the name of *Khillano* (The naughty boy). He was brought up by his uncle as he had lost his parents early. He used to play around with his friends. He was very fond of listening to stories of kings, giants and lions etc. He imagined himself as the hero of that story and travelled to those lands in dreams.

One day he thought of a new plan and started working on it with his friends. They dug up a deep pit outside the village and covered it with dry branches, leaves and grass. When a mare died in the village, they dragged its dead body near the pit. This was the first part of his plan which was completed by all. But now he was to do the job all alone. So he sent them away and sat inside the pit hidden under grass. He had carried a strong rope with him.

After a few hours vultures started coming and flying over the pit. Now started the second part of his plan. Big black vultures with flapping wings came down

and started eating away the dead body. As they came near the pit while eating, *khillano* started tying their feet to one another with the strong rope. After tying them tightly, he held the other corner of the rope in his hand and jumped over the back of a central vulture. After eating to their fill, the vultures rose up to the sky and carried *khillano,* too, on their back.

Oh! What a wonderful experience! *khillano's* eyes were dazed to see the sights. His heart fluttered and spirit soared in that flight. He watched with delight....... the green earth, the serpent-like rivers, high mountains and cities with houses like match-boxes. He had always dreamed of a flight around the world and it has come true. His joy knew no bounds.

He kept on flying for the whole day and covered a long distance. Now he felt the pangs of hunger and thirst. He was also dead tired of sitting on the vulture's back. He wanted to come down on earth. But how to do it? The vultures could not be stopped and brought down to earth. He racked his brains and thought of an idea. He took out his pocket-knife and started cutting off the rope from the vultures' feet. As their feet got free, they flew away leaving only one vulture who carried *Khillano*. Now it started coming down due to its weight. As it neared the ground, *Khillano* jumped down and the vulture flew away.

When *Khillano* touched the ground, he could barely walk with his stiff legs. With continuous sitting, his steps were unsteady. He walked slowly and reached across a field. There was a river which was to be crossed.

There was neither a boat nor someone to help him. He needed to reach some village to get food. He stood helplessly waiting for some help. Suddenly he heard a loud sound like the thunder of clouds. Then he saw a big horse coming with a giant on its back. The giant's body looked like a black mountain and his eyes shone like burning coals. His meter-long moustaches made his face more ferocious. The horse stopped near *Khillano.* He was so scared that he caught at the horse's tail. The giant mounted down the horse and went to the river. He changed the flow of the water to the other side with his large spade. Water rushed with such force that *Khillano* would have been drowned. But he was saved by holding the horse's tail tightly. He looked just like a frog stuck to the ship-size body of the horse. Now the giant mounted up the horse and galloped away. *Khillano,* too, was carried with him. They reached the land of the Giants.

The horse stopped before the door of a big building. The giant got down and knocked at the door. His wife opened the door. She, too, was very huge like her husband. *Khillano,* also entered the room. The room looked like a large store-hall and the roof seemed to touch the sky. *Khillano* hurried to stand in a dark corner. In fact he was too small to be noticed by the giants. Now the couple sat and started eating food. The quantity of food was equal to one month's ration for *Khillano.* After finishing their meal, both retired to their bedroom and the house was filled with the thunderous sound of their snoring.

This made *Khillano* laugh for the first time. It was a strange experience for him. He had only heard the stories of giants but now he was living with them. He was happy as well as afraid. He, too, ate to his fill and rested in the corner.

Thus he began living there as their unseen guest. He enjoyed this but was always very careful. If they notice him, his life would end within a moment. But he was just like a mosquito in the giant's eyes. So he always remained hidden in the dark corner. He had strange experiences every hour. Once he fell into the large milk-pan when he tried to drink milk. He was about to be drowned but the giant's wife noticed it and picked him out thinking it a worm. Poor *Khillano's* body ached for many days due to this fall. He vowed never to try this again. One day she was feeding her giant baby in her lap, when *Khillano* pricked her back with a pin. But it did not hurt her and she dismissed it with just."Oh"!

Many days passed thus. Now *Khillano* felt home-sick. But how to go and where to find the way from this land of the Giants? One day the giant's wife fell ill. The Lama was called to give her medicine. He gave the medicine. It was put in a bucket which was to be drunk twice a day. She took the medicine but did not get well even after two days. The giant was very sad. He loved her so much that his tears filled the buckets which had to be emptied by the servants. This made *Khillano* laugh a lot.

At last the Lama was called again to heal her. He said, "Your house has been desecrated with some foreign living being. The fever will leave only after the expulsion of that thing." So a big worship was prepared by the Lama. On a worship-altar, an idol of a small man was made with barley-flour. Now the Lama started reciting holy-words (Mantras), *Khillano* understood that it would harm and cause his death. He had heard from his uncle that these worship-mantras were capable of killing a foreign being in the house. So he was scared to death. But his uncle had also told him a way to safety. If that idol is broken a little, the worship won't achieve the desired result. So as Lama was reciting 'Mantras' with closed eyes he stepped forward and broke one arm of the idol.

When Lama opened his eyes, he was shocked to see the broken idol. He said that the foreign being was so powerful that only the Head Lama can drive it away. So the Head Lama came with his hundred pupils. Now the worship was performed on a larger scale. The Lama prepared two idols with barley-flour. One idol was of the horse and the other of *Khillano* stuck to its tail. *Khillano* trembled on seeing these. He saw his instant death after the ceremony. He was unable to touch the idols in the presence of so many persons. As the worship was over, the Lama said loudly - "Pick up these idols and throw out."

Then *Khillano* stepped forward and begged for his life weeping - "Please, have pity on me. Do not kill me—. I will go back home.....please!" Suddenly he felf a heavy blow on him and he fell down crying. His eyes were opened and he saw his uncle standing beside his bed, "O' Khillano! Do you sleep or wrestle in the bed? And what were you muttering in sleep – 'let me go home'. You are already at home with your uncle."

❑

Tit for Tat

Once there lived two friends. One was blind and the other humped. Both lived together. As they were unable to earn their livelihood alone, both of them went for begging together. The humped used to watch the blind friend getting more coins than him. As he put more coins into his box at night, the humped felt very jealous of him. So he thought of a plan and said to the blind – "You see, no one gives me coins. How can I make my living without alms? Would you please keep me as your servant?"

The blind one took pity on the humped and told him to cook and work for him. So the humped started living with him. He got up early in the morning, cleaned the hut and cooked food. Thus both had a comfortable life.

But the humped was not satisfied with his lot. His jealousy and greed forced him to play a trick on the blind. One evening while they were returning home after begging, he pushed the blind man from a hillock on way. The poor blind man started falling down like a stone. He struggled to catch some shrub or tree.

Luckily a shrub came into his hand and he called out for help. His cries made the humped take pity on him and he pulled him safe. The blind man heaved a sigh of relief and said, "O humped! Why did you push me down the hill?"

The humped had already manipulated an excuse. He replied – "No brother, I did not push you down. It was a thorn that pricked me on foot and I fell down pushing you too."

The blind kept quiet, but knew at heart that he must be careful of this black sheep.

One day, the humped brought home a dead snake. He had a sinister scheme to cook it and serve it to the blind man as fish. Thus he would die of poison and never come to know of this. He cut the snake into pieces and put it in a pan to cook on fire. Giving the spoon to the blind, he said, "Brother, I am going out for a while. Keep on stirring the dish. When it is cooked, you may eat it and keep my share aside."

He went out imagining the coming event when the blind would meet his end after eating the poisonous dish. His evil mind rejoiced at the thought of having all the coins which belonged to the blind.

Now the blind man started stirring the dish with the spoon. The steam rose to his face and his eyes began to water. After some time, his eyes started seeing— Lo! He could see everything now. He was amazed to have regained his eye-sight. He looked at the pan and shrieked in horror to see the pieces of snake in it, in an instant he understood the humped's evil scheme. Luckily the evil had taken a turn for good to restore his eye-sight. "But that cursed fellow had made an arrangement for my death. Let him come. I will teach him a lesson for life." Thinking thus, he hid behind the door holding a strong stick.

As soon as the humped entered the house at night, the blind stuck him hard with the stick. After beating him black and blue, he shouted, "Now tell me you scoundrel! Why did you plan to kill me with the snake in the dish? It was my good fortune that turned the scale and my lost sight was restored and I was saved."

On hearing this, the humped looked up and tried to justify himself – "Friend, you have again misunderstood my intentions. You see, I had put this snake in order to cure your eye-sight."

The blind man could not be duped now. So he, too, added –"Well, you, too, misunderstood me because I have beaten you to straighten your hump."

Now the humped looked surprised. He got up and jerked himself. Lo! His hump had been straightened. At this miracle, both friends burst into pearls of laughter.

❑

Three for You and Two for Me!

Ramoti Haat was a very small village. It had only six houses where six families lived happily. In one house lived an aged couple. Both were seventy years old. Both loved and cared for each other. They had no son or daughter. But they were contented and lived happily.

One day it rained heavily the whole day. At evening-tea, the husband said, "Listen dear, the weather has turned very pleasant. Let's prepare some *Pakoras*."

The wife replied - "Yes, it is a good idea. But let me see whether there is gram-flour (*Besan*) in the container.

She went to the kitchen and was shocked to see only a little *Besan* in it. She said, "Look, there is only very little *Besan* that may prepare 4-5 *Pakoras* only. But how can you go to the shop now? So let's use this only."

Both prepared the *Besan* adding some onions and made *Pakoras*. Only five *Pakoras* could be prepared.

As she brought them before him, he said - "You know, we always share a new dish with our neighbours. So first serve these to them".

The wife looked perplexed and said – "How can we share these five Pakoras with our neighbours?. There would be none for us then."

The husband understood the problem. After a while he reconciled with her suggestion that she would buy more *Besan* tomorrow and make enough *Pakoras* to be shared by all tomorrow.

Now both sat down to eat *Pakoras*. The wife served three Pakoras in husband's plate and herself took the plate of two *Pakoras*.

As she was about to eat, he said – "Why this difference? You will have only two and I three? Am I such a greedy one?"

The wife smiled – "No, I want you to have three --."

"But I want you to have three.........."

"No, only you would have three and that is final" the wife put a stop to the argument. But the husband proved more adamant. He put his plate before her and insisted – "I will have only two while you have these three *Pakoras*!"

Now this was a case of too much love and care between husband and wife. Each loved the other with more than life and wanted to have equal share. But how could five *Pakoras* be divided equally?

The husband suggested – "Why not break the fifth *Pakora* into two and have equal share?" The wife replied "No, that would spoil the real taste of *Pakoras*."

So the matter could not be decided. The problem remained unsolved. As it had grown quite late. So both decided to go to bed. It was decided that whosoever got up first, would eat three Pakoras. With this decision, they went to sleep.

At morning, both woke up at the same time. But they did not open their eyes and waited for the other to get up first. Time went on and both kept on the drama of sleeping. As the door did not open as usual, the neighbours got suspicious. They knocked and called at the door. But both kept quiet for fear of being the first to get up. They were tied with the condition of self-imposed ban. So the villagers broke open the door. They rushed towards their beds. Both kept lying without opening their eyes. The villagers understood that they had died in sleep.

They started weeping and making preparation to take them to the cremationground. As the coffin etc. was brought and they were about to carry them for putting on the wooden-pyre, the husband opened his eyes and blurted out – "Well, you have two and I have three." As soon as the wife heard these words, she, too, got up and said, "O.K. I will eat two and you three."

On hearing these words from the dead couple, the villagers got horrified. They thought that the couple had turned into ghosts and were talking about eating up the neighbours, so they ran away in panic. The couple burst into a fit of laughter. After sometime they came out and narrated the whole matter to their neighbours and all had a hearty laugh over this funny drama of Pakoras!

❑

Ayodhaya's Ram in Kullu

Once upon a time, King Jagat Singh ruled over Kullu. He was lucky to have everything - his family, wealth and Kingdom, but lacked in good qualities. Notorious for his evil deeds, he punished anyone for anything. He snatched anything which attracted his eye. Nobody's wealth or pretty daughter felt safe in his regime. People were scared of his atrocities. But none could speak against this. How could they complain against the King?

One day, the King came to know of a Brahmin who had one valuable jewel. The greedy King was lured to grab it. He sent for the Brahmin, but the Brahmin was too proud to succumb to the King's demand. His refusal to present himself to the Royal court enraged the King. The Brahmin preferred death, to dishonour at the hands of the cruel King. So he did self-immolation alongwith his family.

Thus the tyrant King suffered a humiliating defeat. Apart from feeling guilty for the death of the entire Brahmin family, the King suffered outwardly too. As he

sat for taking food, he saw worms littering his food. He could not eat even a morsel. The food was again cooked and served to him. But his plate was full of worms always. The King was shocked at the sight. He consulted his wise astrologers. They said - "Your Highness, you have been cursed due to the death of the Brahmin family."

"How can I survive this curse?" In answer to King's question, the Brahmins replied - "This curse can be averted, if Raghunath Chand Rama's idol is brought from Ayodhaya and enthroned as the King in your place."

The King, indeed, was anxious to atone for his sins. So he sent a Pandit to Ayodhaya for this purpose, The Pandit reached Ayodhaya and started to live in Raghunath Temple. He tried hard to get Rama's idol but could not succeed. How could the priests let him have their idol? At last the Pandit stole the idol from the temple and ran away with it. But he was caught on the way. Now there was severe row between the priests of Ayodhaya and priests of Kullu.

At last the solution to this problem was found. The idol was kept between both parties and both were asked to hold it by turn. First, priest of Ayodhaya tried to carry the idol, but could not succeed. The idol was, as if, glued to the Earth. Then, the Priest of Kullu tried to move it and Lo! The idol moved from the Earth and came into his hands.

Now it was clear that even Raghunathji was happy to go to Kullu. The priest returned to his place with the idol of Rama. Ragunath's idol was enthroned with great rejoicings. The King performed holy worship and pledged not to commit those sins again. It was then that he became curse-free. The sacred idols of Lord Rama and other Gods reside in Kullu from that time. There is great celebration in a fair on Dusshera Day as people of Himachal believe that Gods really come to bless the people on that day.

❑

The Wise Rabbit

Once, a rabbit, a crow and a wolf, were travelling together. They saw the dead body of a Lama on the way. Someone must have murdered him. The three friends collected his things and began to distribute among themselves. There was a pair of woollen shoes, one rosary and a packet of food. Neither wolf nor the crow could decide as who should be given the things. So they said to the rabbit – "Friend, you are the wisest of all. Therefore you can distribute the things in a just manner."

The clever rabbit replied – "Friend, being the elder, both of you have the first right. So the woollen shoes should be given to the wolf as he has to run around in cold and snow to look for food. These shoes would keep his feet warm." The wolf was very pleased to get the woollen shoes.

Now it was the crow's turn. The rabbit said – "Friend, you have to fly around in search of food. So this miracle-rosary would prove very useful for you. As the Lama used to know about everything while sitting, so by wearing this rosary, you can know the

whereabouts of food while sitting on a tree." The crow put the rosary in his neck with lots of thanks.

Then the rabbit pointed towards the food packet and said, "I accept this useless packet." The crow and wolf were very impressed with the rabbit's humility. All bade farewell to one another and went to their places.

The rabbit opened the food packet and was overjoyed to see food. He enjoyed that food for many days. When winter set in, the wolf put on his woollen shoes. He felt very warm and comfortable. He walked through the snowy path with great ease. But he had hardly gone a little far when he stumbled and fell down. The reason was his woollen shoes. Not to talk of running, he could barely walk with those shoes. He tried hard to put his feet firmly and walk, but in vain. In this attempt, he slipped down a stone and fell tumbling down into a gorge. His life was saved but he got hurt seriously. Cursing the rabbit, he threw away the shoes and resolved to take revenge on him.

The crow, too, suffered similarly. He wore the rosary and sat on a tree to wait for some miracle. But nothing happened. At last he flew in search of food, but his rosary got stuck in a branch. It tightened around his neck. The more he tried to free it, the more it grew tight. He feared that it would strangle him to death. So he struggled hard and got himself free from it. He was furious and decided to punish the rabbit for this.

After a few days, the wolf and the crow met in the forest. Each narrated his bitter experience to the other. Both were determined to teach a lesson to the clever rabbit. Luckily they succeeded to find him in the forest. The rabbit, too, saw them at a distance. As he looked at their faces, he understood that something was wrong. So he immediately hit his face against a rock and lay down, crying with pain.

The wolf and the crow went near the rabbit and shouted – "O clever rabbit! Get up. Now we know about your shrewdness. You cheated us. Get ready now to be punished severely."

The rabbit raised his head with a cry and moaned – "Friends, how would I cheat you when I myself was a prey to deception. Look at my face and bruised nose. I was wounded when the dacoits tried to snatch that damned food from me. They beat me so hard that I have been suffering with pain for so many days."

Both believed on that made up story and put the blame on their bad luck. So the clever rabbit was saved from their wrath once again.

❑

Three Valuable Advices

Once, a King gave exile to his son as punishment for some offence. Before sending him away, he gave him three lac rupees. Now the prince left the palace and travelled to far off land to try his luck. As he passed through a forest, he saw a strange saint who spoke in a loud voice – "One can have a valuable advice worth one lac rupees." The prince was surprised and thought – "It must be a rare advice that costs one lac rupees. I should try to get it."

He approached the saint and requested – "Respected Saint, kindly accept this money and give me the valuable advice."

The Saint accepted the money and gave this advice into his ear – "Son, you should never sleep on another's bed before dusting it off." The prince heard and repeated it in his mind.

When he was about to leave, the saint said, "I possess two more valuable advices but you have to pay two lac rupees for that." The prince was impressed by the saint's wisdom so he was ready to have those two more advices. He gave two lac rupees to the saint

and received these lessons – First advice was – "Never eat anything given by strangers." Second was – "The relatives are true to you till you are rich."

The prince started on his journey enriched with three valuable advices but like a beggar without even one rupee. Now he had only these three advices to support and save him and his own strength of body and mind. It was getting dark in the forest. He looked for some shelter at night. He saw a hut at a distance. As he reached it, an old lady welcomed him inside. He was dead tired. So he asked for only a bed to sleep for the night. The lady made a bed for him in a corner. When he was about to lie down, he remembered the saint's advice – "Never sleep on another's bed before dusting it off." So he uncovered the bed and was horrified to see that there was no bed underneath it but a deep pit. Had he lain on the bed, he would have fallen in it! Now he understood that the old lady must be a witch who wanted to eat him up. He thanked the saint for saving his life.

He cut off the witch's head and left that hut. He reached a small village. As he felt hungry, he approached a house. There was a woman with her daughter. He asked for food. They welcomed him inside and prepared food for him. As he was about to eat the first morsel of bread, the second advice of the saint flashed in his mind. He gave the first morsel to a cat sitting beside him. No sooner had the cat swallowed the food, it fainted and died. The prince was shocked at the horrible sight. The saint had saved him from death again. He immediately left the place.

Now he reached a village where his sister lived with her family. He stayed in an inn and sent for his sister to meet him. But she did not come to meet him. Perhaps she had become aware of his brother's poor condition due to exile.

This proved that third advice, too, was worth the sum of money. The prince got the shock of his life that every relation is bound with wealth only.

The prince was wiser now after experiencing all this. He resumed his journey to another village. At last he reached a state whose king had expired and there was a search for a capable person to be crowned. There was one condition. The royal elephant stood at the gate of the city. When it would hold a person by its trunk and mount him over itself, he would be crowned as King. As the prince neared the elephant, it caught him with its trunk and put him over his seat. All rejoiced to see this sight. It was a decree in favour of the prince. He was taken to the Royal Court and crowned as the King of the state. At last the prince received the honourable reward he deserved.

❑

The Charismatic Guests

It was a rainy night in winter. Lord Vishnu and Goddess Lakshmi planned to visit the Earth at such an odd hour. In fact, they wanted to test a human being. So they came down the Earth in the guise of a poor couple. They saw a big house on the way and knocked at the door. The owner of the house opened the door. As he looked at them, he understood that they must be beggars. He spoke with dislike – "Go away. This is not an inn for the beggars." Saying this, he shut the door.

The poor couple stood helpless in the torrential rain. Suddenly they noticed a small hut nearby. They went to it and knocked at the door. The housewife immediately answered the call with a lamp in her hand. Looking at them she said with a smile, "Please come in. You are drenched to the core, please come inside."

As they entered the hut, both understood that it belonged to the very poor. It had only two cots, some tattered clothes and a few utensils. Putting a clean sheet on the cot, she made them sit and brought some clothes

from inside. She said, "These old clothes are not worthy of you, still change into these dry clothes." Leaving both to change their clothes, she went inside to prepare food for them. She served them food, saying, "Guest is like God for me. But I only have these *Rotis of Bajra* for you. Please accept this simple food."

Just then, her husband entered with a load of firewood on his head. As he saw the guests, he was very happy. He touched their feet with respect and helped his wife in serving them food. After meal, the guests were requested to sleep on their beds while the couple slept on the floor.

The guests got ready to leave next morning. The couple had already prepared breakfast and packed some *rotis* for their journey. The guests were overwhelmed with a feeling of love and gratitude for the affectionate couple. They blessed them saying – "Your true service has earned a reward for you. Whatever you start doing today, would continue till evening."

After their departure, the poor woman took the pot to clean, but she was surprised to see it full of gold muhars (coins). She emptied the pot, but it was full again. She emptied it again, but it was filled with gold coins again. Both were amazed at this miracle. Now they understood that it was a boon given by those Godly guests. This miracle continued till evening as promised by God. Now they became the richest couple in one day. Thanking God for this fortune, they bought a big house and a cloth shop. Now they started living a life of comfort and luxury.

The rich neighbour was very jealous of the poor couple's sudden shower of fortune. He called them to his house and asked about the source of this good luck. The simpleton couple narrated the whole incident to the rich man. Now the rich man realized his blunder and repented at his foolishness. He hoped against hope that those miraculous guests might come again. He was lucky. One rainy night, the same guests knocked at his door. Now, he was ready to welcome them with a smile. He took them inside with great respect. His wife brought them dry clothes to change. She could offer them new clothes, but she gave them the old worn clothes. Now she prepared *Bajra Rotis* for them. She could have served them the best food but both were so blinded with greed that they copied the poor couple in everything. In fact their aim was not to serve the guests but to get gold from them.

After this the guests were made to sleep on their beds while they slept on the floor. They could not sleep for the whole night because they were anxious to possess gold coins. In the morning they prepared *Bajra Rotis* for them and stood waiting for the desired boon.

God Vishnu and Goddess Lakshmi were very amused at this. Lord said – "Your wish would be granted. Whatever you start doing today, would continue till evening." On hearing this, both were beside themselves with joy. They had succeeded in getting the desired boon. They ran to open the lid of the pan. Both were too excited to let the other open it. They started quarrelling with each other. Each argued to have the first claim to open the lid of the pan. At last the wife succeeded to have the first right. As soon as she opened the lid of the pan, she saw the left-over dish in it. Because, she had not served the whole dish to the guests, due to her greed. So she emptied the pan to clean it, the pan was filled again with the left-over dish. She was shocked to see the left-over again. And there was no sign of even a single gold coin.

She ran to call her husband. Both again prayed to God and emptied the pan again. It was the same left-over dish in the pan once more. Both went mad at this. This went on till the evening. They got dead tired and the room was filled with the left-over dish. They cursed themselves for their foolishness. Now they understood that they had been punished for their greed and ill-will for the poor guests. God had dispensed justice to the greedy rich couple.

❑

Maina Speaks the Truth

Once there lived a princess – lovely like a doll and pretty like a fairy. Her heart was as soft as butter and mind was as clear as the water of the lake. Her parents loved her very much. Her smile was bewitching and she talked sweetly. She had one close friend who accompanied her to the temple daily. Both offered prayers and a gold and a silver coin to the priest. When the princess offered him a gold coin, he blessed her – "You will marry a corpse." As her friend offered a silver coin, he said, "You will marry a prince."

Strange were the priest's blessings to both. As long as they were small, they did not care to notice it. But when they grew up and began to understand the meaning, they felt very upset. The princess kept thinking – "Why am I cursed to marry a corpse? Why this injustice to me? She felt very sad. She lost her zest in life. Now she neither ate nor dressed like before. She forgot to sing and smile even. In fact, she was no longer that lovely princess, but only a shadow of her former self.

The King and the Queen were pained to see this. They knew at heart that the priest's prophecy never went wrong. This aggravated their grief. The King too lost interest in his court-work. Both devised many ways to entertain their daughter, but all was in vain.

One day the King took the princess for a ride in the forest. The princess felt happy after a long time. She smiled in the refreshing company of the trees, flowers and birds. The calm and beautiful surroundings made her forget her grief. The King felt pleased to see her talking and laughing as before. They spent the whole day enjoying themselves.

As evening fell, the King mounted the horse with her daughter and started homeward. But it grew dark and they lost the way. Helpless to stay in the forest, they looked for some place to stay at night. Suddenly, the princess saw a house at a distance. Both heaved a sigh of relief and reached the house. It was a big building. As the princess knocked the door, the door opened. She entered happily with the King following her with the horse. But as soon as the princess got in, the door closed. The King hurried and pushed the door, but the door was sealed tightly. The King knocked and pushed it with all his might but it did not budge. The princess too tried to open it from inside but to no avail. They called out loudly for help but none replied. There was no one in sight. Then who opened and closed the door? Both stood helpless alone- daughter inside, father outside. Their efforts and cries were useless. The King cried for his daughter and the princess cried for her father. But they could not meet. The whole night was spent in deep anguish.

As the day dawned, the princess was surprised to see that it was a great palace. It had many rooms and gardens. She went inside with a trembling heart. But she saw none anywhere. Every room was well furnished and decorated with valuable things. The almirahs were full of royal dresses and the kitchen had everything to eat. She went from one room to another wondering at that strange place. But her surprise turned into shock when she saw a dead body lying on a royal bed in a room. Se shrieked with horror. After controlling herself, she looked at it again. It was the dead body of a handsome prince who seemed to be in deep sleep. There was no sign of blood or injury on the body. But it had wild grass grown over it.

She stood gazing and wondering at that strange sight. What does this mean? Who was he? Why was he looking like a corpse? There was none to answer her questions. Suddenly its meaning dawned on her like a lightening in the clouds. It was the same corpse with whom she was to be married as the priest had predicted. So the destiny had willed it and she was forced to enter the palace alone.

Now she sat down and said to herself – "If it is my destiny, I have to accept it. Neither can I go out nor can anyone enter the palace. So I'll make it my home. I have to live here all alone." Her father too returned to his kingdom after waiting at the closed gate for three days.

The princess went to sleep with a heavy heart, she had a dream. A Godly voice spoke thus – "Daughter, don't be afraid of this dead body. Have patience and follow this routine. Get up before sunrise, have bath and worship the Sun God. After this, pull out one strand of grass from this dead body daily. When you have pulled out the last strand of grass, this dead body would come to life and you would have your bridegroom."

The princess was overjoyed after having this dream. Her mind at rest, she started following the routine daily. Now her days began to pass happily. She pulled out one strand of grass that had grown over the dead body after worshipping Sun God. This went on for many days. But she believed and waited patiently. One day a trader passed that way. He knocked at the gate to get some water. Strangely enough, now the gate opened. The princess gave him water. He had his daughter with him. She reminded the princess of her own friend. So she requested the trader to leave his daughter with her. Luckily the trader agreed to it. Now the princess spent her days with great pleasure alongwith her friend.

The trader's daughter watched the princess doing her morning routine and wondered about this ritual. She asked her about it. The princess told her everything in good faith. But that girl was not innocent like her. She had an evil mind. So she devised a scheme to deceive her. When there remained only one strand of grass on the corpse, she got up earlier than the princess. After worshipping the Sun God, she pulled out the last strand of grass and lo! The dead prince came back to life.

The prince's eyes fell on the girl and it was love at first sight. Both exchanged garlands and got married in an instant. They were engrossed in merry gossip, when the princess came there. She had come to pull out the last strand of the grass and meet her bridegroom. But she was shocked to see both sitting as newly married. She understood the vicious plan of the girl who had cleverly snatched her bridegroom. The girl introduced the princess to the prince as her servant. The princess was shaken with the blow of cruel destiny. But what cannot be cured must be endured. So she bowed before her fate and started her life as a servant of the house. Now that girl lived a life of luxury as the princess and the princess led a life of misery as the servant.

Days and weeks went on like this. One day the prince went out for some purchase. He asked both of them if they needed something from the bazaar. The trader's daughter gave a long list of clothes and cosmetics to be bought while the princess asked only for a bird Maina.

When the prince came back in the evening, he gave each her favourite things. The princess was overjoyed to get that bird. She felt as if her friend had come back to share her sorrow. Whenever she was free from work, she sat down with the bird and narrated her own story to the bird. Her grieving heart received solace after unburdening her grief. The bird seemed to be listening and sympathizing with her. The trader's daughter noticed this and tried to snatch the bird from her. But the prince intervened and let the bird remain with the princess.

One day, the trader's daughter complained against the bird to the prince. She wanted to kill it because it spoke false tales about her. The prince wanted to get the proof. So he got the bird into his room and asked Maina to tell the whole story. He knew that a Maina never tells a lie.

Now the Maina started to narrate the true story of the princess. When the story reached the last stage, where the trader's daughter cheated the princess by pulling out the last strand of grass from the corpse, the trader's daughter pounced upon the bird to kill it. But the bird flew to the wall and completed the story. Now the prince knew everything. The princess' tears and the girl's anger gave ample proof for that. He was so enraged that he drew out his sword to kill the trader's daughter. But the princess begged him to pardon her life. The girl admitted having committed the crime. The prince granted her life and let her go away. Now he took his true wife and went to visit his in-laws. The King and the Queen were overjoyed to see their daughter married to the real prince and blessed them.

❑

Son versus Stone

Once, there was a King who was very kind, just and hard-working. People were happy and prosperous. But the King could not feel happy, because he had no son or daughter. He had married seven times but was not blessed with a child. So he married the eighth time. Now lady-luck smiled over him. The eighth Queen got pregnant. The King's joy knew no bounds. The whole kingdom rejoiced over this good news. Special worship-functions were held and all celebrated the good news with great enthusiasm. The King took great care to look after the Queen.

As the lucky day drew near, the seven Queens became restless with jealousy. They were not happy at all. They imagined their dark future when the eighth Queen would give birth to a son.

At last they got united to hatch a conspiracy against the eighth Queen. They went to the King with this request – "Your Highness! The royal family is going to be blessed with a prince after such a long time. So we don't want to take any risk with the Queen's safe

delivery. Therefore, we have planned to do this delivery by ourselves. We shall look after our sister and won't allow any mid-wife to touch her."

The King being a noble man felt pleased with his seven Queens and accepted their proposal happily. On the appointed day, the Queen gave birth to a son. The shrewd Queens had already told the eighth Queen that it was decreed by the priest that the mother should not look at her new-born to avoid some bad omen. So they had blind-folded her and given her a dose of medicine. So she could neither see nor hear her son after delivery. For fear of the child's safety she did not ask to see her son even after gaining consciousness. The seven Queens were so vicious that they replaced the child with a stone and took the child away.

When the King came to have a look at his child, the Queens cried and said – "Your Highness! We had prayed for a son, but could only get this stone. The Queen is no less than a witch who has given birth to a stone."

On seeing the stone, the King was shocked. It was a bolt from the blue. He went mad with grief and anger and ordered the eighth Queen to be made a servant as punishment. This was what the seven Queens had wanted. They were overjoyed with the success of their plan.

Now, what happened to that child? The cruel Queens handed over the child to a servant and told him to throw it in front of a snake. The servant obeyed the order. But the snake proved kinder; it did not bite the child and crept away. Then, they threw it before an elephant, but the elephant, too, refused to trample the child under its foot. It appeared as if some unseen hands were protecting the child. But those evil Queens were bent upon killing the child, so they put the child in a wooden-box and threw it in the river.

The box fell into the hands of a fisherman. When he opened the box, he was surprised to see a beautiful child. He was overjoyed to be blessed with this boon from God. He took it home and gave it to his wife. Both of them brought him up like their own son. The child showed all signs of royalty. Besides physical strength and beauty, he was very active in archery. He aimed so perfectly at the animals that he was called Gole which meant a perfectionist in taking aim. He was also aware of his royal birth and knew everything regarding his parents.

One day, he chanced to hunt near the river that bordered his father's kingdom. He saw the Queens coming to the river with their pitchers. When they were about to leave after filling their pitchers, Gole aimed at their pitchers and they broke into pieces. Only the eighth pitcher remained intact because Gole had aimed at it with a flower. The seven Queens went away complaining and crying.

Next day they again came to fill water into their pitchers. Today Gole had come there with his wooden horse. When the Queens were about to fill their pitchers, he came forward and said, "Let my horse drink water first". The seven Queens laughed in mockery. "How can a wooden horse drink water?" but Gole was adamant. As they tried to fill their pitchers, he broke them but did not harm the eighth Queen's pitcher. He helped her fill it and put it on her head. At this the seven Queens became very angry and went to the King's court to complain against him. The King sent his men to bring the boy to the court.

When Gole was brought before the King, he said in anger, "Hey Boy, why did you break the Queens' pitchers?" Gole replied fearlessly – "Your Highness, they did not let my horse drink water first. You know the thirsty horse needed water immediately while they could fill their pitchers later."

The King laughed at the boy's funny argument and said, "Stupid Boy! Can a wooden horse be thirsty and drink water?"

Now, Gole, too, smiled and replied, "Your Majesty, if a Queen can give birth to a stone, then a wooden horse can also drink water."

Gole's words rang in the Court-Hall and everyone was shocked to understand the hidden meaning. The Eighth Queen listened from behind a curtain. Now she came into the court and embraced her son. The King understood the truth behind his words. Now the eighth Queen narrated the whole story to the King. He was shocked to know the conspiracy hatched by the seven Queens. He ordered all to be sentenced to death immediately. But Gole requested his father to pardon their crime and grant them life. So the King punished them by expelling them from the kingdom. After this,

Gole was made the crown-prince. The King transferred his power to his son and all lived a happy life. Gole King is a very popular name in the hilly stories till today.

❑

The Ghost's Gown

Once upon a time a ghost disturbed the peace of a small village in the valley. It was very shrewd and troubled the innocent villagers with its tricks. It did not kill or beat them but irritated them with strange pranks. Sometimes it put red pepper in cooking dish or put water in the pot of milk. Sometimes it threw water in the burning stove or lighted fire in a cool stove. The poor people were fed up with these troubles and wanted to punish it. But, how to catch it? It was unseen and so could not be caught.

One day the ghost played a horrible trick with the headman of the village. It shaved off his beard while he was asleep. When he woke up, he was beside himself with rage at the loss of his beard. How dare the ghost insult him like this? He called an urgent meeting of the villagers and decided that the ghost should be awarded severe punishment. So the Head Lama was requested to help them. He was the panacea for all ills. The villagers called him *Chela* (disciple) of God. The Lama came in the morning and started ceremonial

worship in the courtyard of the Headman. The ghost was entrapped by the power of the holy-mantras (words). It struggled hard to free itself and was able to flee from the house but the Lama rushed to catch it. He could only clutch at its gown. The ghost disappeared in air.

The villagers heaved a sigh of relief. The '*Chela*' (Lama) was awarded with many gifts. Now none had to suffer at the hands of the ghost. In fact, the tables had been turned over the ghost itself. As the ghost's gown was in 'Chela's' house, so the ghost was in his control. It begged for its gown but the '*Chela*' replied, "First plough my fields or water my fields or chop the wood, etc." The ghost did everything. It was always at the beck and call of the Lama. Now he rested at home while the ghost worked outside. The Lama was now a king and the ghost his slave. As long as its gown was in his custody, the ghost was in prison.

So it approached another senior ghost to help it free itself from the Lama. The senior ghost promised to bring back its gown. It went to that village and waited for the opportunity. As the Lama went to the river for a bath, the ghost went to his house in the guise of a shepherd. It knocked at the door and was greeted by Lama's wife. The ghost said, "I am your husband's old friend. I have brought butter and cheese from my home for you." As it gave these things to her, she was immensely pleased. She served tea and snacks to it. When it got up to leave, she said, "Why don't you stay for the night and meet your friend?"

The shepherd replied, "No, I cannot stay as I have to look after my sheep which are grazing in the forest. Please convey my regards to my friend. Well I had forgotten my gown here last time. Would you please find it and give it back to me?"

"Yes, let me see.." saying this, she went to the kitchen and brought the ghost's gown. The shepherd took it immediately and was gone. When the Lama returned in the evening, his wife narrated the whole story. As she mentioned the gown, the Lama was startled. He rushed to the kitchen where the gown was hung. It was not there. He cursed his luck and lamented - "Oh! We are doomed." His wife said in surprise, "What was special in that dirty gown? Look, your friend bought us home-made butter and cheese." She went to the kitchen to get those. But there was no sign of cheese and butter. They, too, had disappeared in thin air. Looking at her fallen face, the Lama said, "You have been proved stupid by the clever ghost. It cheated you and took away its gown, which was serving us like a slave day and night."

Now the Lama had to do all those jobs himself. Both worked in the fields, chopped wood and fetched water. They missed those good old days when the ghost used to do all this.

❑

Chandar Taal

Surrounded by snow-clad mountains, the lake of Chandar Taal was sparkling like a diamond ring in the valley. Spring was coming and the snow on the mountains was melting. New buds of plants had sprouted from the earth. Green grass had encircled the lake from all round. This was an open invitation for the shepherds to come with their herd of sheep.

Kishna was a shepherd boy. He lived in the valley with his brother and *Bhabhi* (sister-in-law). As his parents had died early, he was brought up by them. But they did not treat him like their brother but like a servant. He worked hard doing various jobs like taking out the cattle to graze, fetching water from a distance, felling and chopping the wood and bringing it home. But he was given only dry bread with harsh words by his *Bhabhi*. This made him sad. He spent his days sighing and waiting for the spring. Because when spring came, he left for the lake with his sheep. After reaching Chandar Taal he felt as if he were in his loving mother's lap.

This year, too, he reached the lake accompanied with his sheep and loyal dog Moti. He kept his rations in the usual place at a cave and let the sheep graze freely escorted by Moti. He took his flute and sat down at the bank of the lake. It was an enchanting scene. Snowy peaks of the Himalayas seemed to be looking at themselves in the crystal-clear water of the lake. Little flowers were smiling at him. The beautiful nature worked like soothing balm over his sore heart. Overwhelmed with pleasure he put the flute to his lips and sweet notes filled the air with music.

When the sheep had grazed for the whole day, Kishna took them into the cave. He prepared his simple *Rotis* and ate these sharing with Moti. Then he closed the entry of the cave with a stone and came to sit on the bank of the lake. It was a moon-lit night. Full moon was reflected in the still water of the lake. A sweet silence prevailed all round. Kishna's heart was filled with ecstasy. He began to sing through his flute. Sweet music echoed in the air. Just then someone called – "Kishna ......" He was startled to hear his name. He looked all around but who could be there to know him in this lonely place? It must be his imagination. But again he heard his name being called and someone touched his shoulder.

Kishna got up and turned his face. Lo! There stood a pretty girl! She looked dazzling like the Moon. Kishna rubbed his eyes. Was it true or a dream? The girl offered her hand and spoke in a musical voice "Kishna! I am the fairy of Chandar Taal. I have known you since you first came here. I used to watch you hidden from view. Your flute sounded very sweet in my ears. When you went back, I would wait for your return. I love you Kishna. I have always loved you very much."

Kishna stood mesmerized listening to her sweet words. It was too good to be true. He was struck dumb with joy and surprise. The fairy held his hand and said – "Come Kishna, come with me. I shall take you to my fairyland -- come!" She took him with her and walked on water as if she were walking on the ground. And Kishna, too, could walk along her! All of a sudden, steps appeared in the centre of the lake and both stepped down and reached the fairyland !

Kishna was dazed to see the palace. It had glittery golden roofs, silvery walls with jewels decorating them. Pretty fairy-maids came to welcome them. They took Kishna to the bathroom and bathed him with scented soap and water. He was given the best silken dress. As he looked into the mirror, he could not recognize himself. His whole self had undergone a change. Now he, too, looked like a handsome prince.

He was served the most delicious food. He was entertained with song and dance. After spending a blissful night with the fairy, he returned in the morning. Bidding him good-bye, the fairy said, "Kishna, I shall come again at night. Be ready." Leaving him spell-bound, she disappeared in the lake.

Kishna spent the whole day lost in her sweet memory. He kept on thinking about the previous night. He could hardly believe that lady-luck had smiled over him. But with the evening came his sweetheart to take him along to the fairyland. He was given a rousing welcome like the previous night. He enjoyed himself with all the comforts. He felt himself to be in heaven having the best time of his life with his beloved fairy.

Thus six months passed but these seemed like six nights only to Kishna. When the first snowfall appeared, he felt very sad. It was a signal for him to leave Chandar Taal. Even the thought of separation from the fairy was unbearable to his heart. The fairy, too, felt sad at his going away. For Kishna, the memory of his cruel *Bhabhi* pricked his heart like a razor. At last, he bade his beloved good-bye with a heavy heart. She said with tears in her eyes – "Kishna, I shall wait for you daily. My night of six months would end when you come back. Do not forget me and never mention my name to anyone." Kishna promised to do so and went to his village with a heavy heart.

Kishna passed these six months in the sweet memories of the past. He counted days and nights with a hopeful heart. When summer arrived, he was the happiest to leave for Chandar Taal. He was overjoyed to meet his beloved fairy in the evening and enjoyed himself in the fairyland as before. In this way many months passed. But for Kishna there was only one season of spring only. He lived only for those six months. The other six months of winter were spent in waiting for the spring. Now he always remained happy. His *Bhabhi's* harsh words could not hurt him now. One day as he sat lost in fairy's memory, *Bhabhi* called –

"Kishna, get up and chop the wood." Kishna was so lost in his thoughts that he did not hear her. She got so angry that she thundered over his head – "O' Kishna, cannot you hear me? Whose memory has made you so forgetful? Have you found the fairy of Chandar Taal? I think, now she would serve you with delicious food."

Bhabhi's sarcastic remarks hurt krishna's sad heart. He lost his patience and these words slipped from his mouth, "Yes, I have found the fairy of Chandar Taal and her dishes are far far superior to the cattle-feed cooked by you."

Kishna's reply struck her like lightning. It shocked her but the shock was greater to Kishna. He was horrified at this slip of the tongue. He was grief-stricken and wailed – "Ah! What have I done? I broke my promise to the fairy...." He rushed to the temple and begged to God – "Oh God, forgive me for my sin....forgive me." He wept for a long time. After that moment, he passed his days and nights immersed in deep sorrow. He counted the days which seemed endless.

He was so restless to reach Chandar Taal that he did not wait for the winter to end. He got ready to leave for the lake before the snow had melted down. Everyone forbade him to travel in such a cold weather. No other shepherd was leaving with his sheep. But Kishna did not listen to anyone. He started with his flock braving frost and icy-cold winds on the way. Many of his sheep died due to severe cold. But Kishna did not stop. He was desperate to reach the lake and meet his beloved.

At last he reached his destination. The lake was still under a thin cover of snow. But the beauty and tranquillity of Chandar Taal soothed his grieving heart. He kept himself busy with the sheep in the day. As evening fell, he drove them into the cave and came to the bank of the lake. It was freezing cold. He kept sitting and waiting for that sweet voice. But there was no sign of the fairy. His heart was full of hope and despair. Anxiety tore his heart with the question – "Has she come to know of my breach of trust? Is she angry with me? Would she never come to meet me?" These thoughts turned him mad with sorrow. He put his flute to his lips and began to sing the notes of love. The heart-rending sound of the flute implored – "Oh, my beloved, come to me.............forgive me..........punish me but come to me......... do not forsake me ....I cannot live without you........come my beloved."

But she did not come. Kishna sat in the freezing cold for the whole night. His legs became numb with cold. His only companion was his faithful Moti who encircled his legs with his own insilent sympathy. In the morning Kishna made himself busy with the sheep. He could neither eat nor sleep. He waited desperately for the night when he hoped to meet his beloved.

At evening, he went to the lake and prayed to God, "Please, send my love to me......forgive my sin and have pity on me." But time passed and all his prayers proved futile. His hopes were dashed to the ground. Kishna sighed and wept but there was none to console him. He waited for another night. But when she did not come on the third night too, his lovelorn heart broke into pieces. His world turned pitch dark. There was no silver lining in his black clouds. Kishna resolved to go himself to meet her. So he put on his white woollen blanket, held the flute in his hand and looked at his sheep and Moti for the last time. He stepped into the lake. He felf as if his beloved held him in her embrace and took him to the deep waters. Poor Moti kept moaning while gazing at the lake.

❑❑❑